Seasons of the Heart

Time and Extreme hardship
can destroy or help love grow.

Edith Webster

SEASONS of the HEART

Castle book
Sequel to A Beggars Worth book

PROLOGUE

The forest and fields surrounding the castle lay smothered in dense fog, sifting in layers, spires and turrets hidden in the early morning mist.

The west wind swept inland from the sea and with it came a covering of forlorn dampness. The trees, now almost bare, were not the longed-for protection by those stranded in the dark.

The stone fence around the castle lands became invisible in places, only outlines of the spiked gate along the rock walls could be seen. Not a night for man nor beast to be without shelter through the night.

But one such unfortunate human lay in the thick fog outside the castle's stone wall. She lay crumpled in the cold dampness against the iron gate leading into the garden. The light cloak covering her could not hold the warmth needed to keep her alive through this last blast of winter. If the near-death soul thought at all, she knew she would not live long. How she happened to be here, at this gate, was a mystery. Weak and confused, unable to move, she surrendered, letting all reason leave.

As her body became weaker, she slipped into oblivion.

The blades of grass, topped with ice crystals, bent low in the cold breeze, barely moving as dawn approached. The frost now covering the gray stone wall and iron gate warned of the coming spring, but just not yet. Late snow could yet cover this part of the world for one last storm. No matter. To the one crumpled by the gate nothing mattered, nothing at all. All dreams were crushed, ending here.

CHAPTER 1

The breeze softened as the morning sunlight spilled over the land, pushing back the night. The young husband stood in the doorway of their cottage, soaking up the first bit of warmth this late-winter morning.

Henri called to his wife, "I see Max coming. Are we late or is he early?"

Sophie laughed, "Max may be many things but being early is not one of them." She slipped on her cloak as Henri stepped out the door of the cottage onto the small porch to greet his friend.

Clasping hands, the two men showed obvious pleasure at being together again before Max turned to wink at Sophie. The young wife laughed. Max was a good friend to Henri, but always a flirt. These two friends lived through some difficult times in the past when they traveled on trips outside of their castle protection. Hunger and pain seemed to abound outside the castle walls. Their trips into the wilderness were made often to bring a basket of food and hope to those still living out in the dark. It was a labor of love. Both men knew they were some of the lucky ones and were happy to help, when possible, any who were still out in the dark.

Henri and Max came on their own, during different seasons, to the castle where they found friendship, and along the way, purpose. Real purpose. Sometimes messy, not always easy, but both men were filled with satisfaction knowing they were helping. Yes, these two men were more than friends.

The wink and smile from the handsome young man with tousled dark curls, bright eyes and deep dimples seemed harmless to those around him. Max always lifted spirits with just a smile and wink before he moved on with his day. But for some, (like Sophie at first, just hours out of the darkness), the wink brought fear. She could not trust anything or anyone in her earliest days at the castle, even though she was told she was safe with Abba and the one called Mary Elizabeth. People could lie, she knew that to be true from her months out in the dark world.

No, Sophie did not feel safe in the beginning. Especially with the handsome charmer called Max.

Sophie's first spring in the safety of the castle turned to summer before she could look directly at Max and smile. Of course, that was months later. At first the young man's behavior forced memories of the past she hoped to forget. Something about that first wink left Sophie pulling back, feeling a slice of fear. All things that looked and seemed acceptable and even felt good in the most human way could destroy the protected feeling that came gently, gradually, over time by just being safe in the castle. In the months that followed her arrival at the castle, Sophie did felt safe. Perhaps for the first time in her life, the young woman felt out of harm's way. Over time Sophie grew to love Max as Henri loved him.

Max, (short for Maximillian), was Henri's dearest friend.

Sophie stepped out to stand by Henri and smiled to welcome Max on this chilly morning.

Today the three were out for their morning trek from their cottage to the castle, some distance through the gardens, to meet friends inside for tea and fresh baked scones. As they walked and spoke of mundane things, Max suddenly stopped mid-stride, causing Henri to bump into him. Henri put his arm out to protect Sophie from being startled.

"What?" Henri stopped, turned his head toward the north wall to see what Max was looking at, anxious to get out of the cold morning air and inside the castle. What or who had caught his friend's attention?

Max, continuing to look toward the rock wall, "I see something beside the iron gate. Wait just a minute while I jog over and check it out."

The heavy iron gate on the side of the castle gardens stood closed. It was used primarily for easy access for those living in the castle or on the castle grounds who were planning a trip to check on the sick or carry a food basket to nearby hamlets.

Henri seemed perplexed that Max glanced in that direction before jogging toward the gate and even now stood waiting for his friends to join him.

Max, not easily excited, waved his arm, motioning his need for them to come quickly.

As he looked, Henri could see something red against the gate that did not seem to belong, something not there yesterday.

Max called, "Come. I need your help here."

Henri and Sophie moved swiftly to the gate, now pushed partially open, to find Max bent over the form of a young woman, too lightly covered to have been protected from the cold night. Her skin was pale, almost translucent, a heavy mass of red hair flowed free from under a scarf once tied under her chin, her eyes closed.

Sophie's heart filled with compassion, "She looks all but starved. Is she alive?" Sophie knelt beside Max and removed her own heavy cloak to cover the young woman.

Max looked up at his tall friend, Henri, who now bent over Sophie, both men remembered another soul, (who was now a close friend to both), found out on a different cold night months earlier. Catching the glance, Henri knew both men remembered the night they found Benjamin.

CHAPTER 2

An involuntary tremble shook Max as he turned all his attention to the young woman, "She is alive. Barely. Help me carry her into the castle. Abba will know what to do." Max gently gathered the girl in his arms as Sophie held the gate and Henri searched the ground around the fence to make sure no possessions were missed. He found a small satchel and picking it up he hurried after Max as the three moved quickly toward the castle carrying the near dead girl.

A friend saw them coming while standing near one of the castle portals and sent someone to tell Abba, then held a side entrance open for them. Max carried the nearly dead soul inside, followed by Sophie and Henri.

The beautiful Mary Elizabeth arrived in a few minutes through a side hallway entrance, "Come this way." Spoken in a soft direct way, turning and with a slight wave, motioned for them to follow her. With a special quiet authority (given to her by Abba overtime), Mary Elizabeth led the small group to a room warmed by a blazing fireplace, well lighted by candles in tall stands.

Max carried the unconscious young woman into the room after being assured by Mary that they were following Abba's wishes. Max placed her carefully on a small cot. Two women, Bridget and Monika, came to help and began to place burlap wrapped heated stones at the new arrivals feet and massaged her hands.

As life blood began to once again flow into her hands and feet, the girl opened her eyes for an instant and whispered, "Joel."

With a slight smile, Mary Elisabeth nodded and whispered, "We will take care of Joel," before adding, "And what is your name?" With slender fingers, Mary pushed hair from the girl's brow and waited for an answer. The eyes closed again, hiding obvious pain, fear, and confusion.

While waiting for the girl to wake up, Mary asked Sophie to run for a cup of warm broth and fresh water. When Sophie returned the girl once again opened her eyes. They held no light. The green eyes were dull and empty except for some unidentified painful memory. Was she hurt or in some mental anguish? Too soon to be determined. No answers yet. Sophie and Mary Elizabeth would wait; answers would come in time. The woman, (difficult to determine age in her disheveled condition), could not or would not drink. Mary did not try to force her.

As Sophie returned to the room where Mary kept watch over the patient, with cool water, Henri and Max followed another friend, Darla, who carried in a tray with a pot of hot tea and warm biscuits. Mary touched her shoulder and mouthed "Thank you."

Darla with her usual warm countenance simply nodded.

"Is there anything else we can do before we go?" Max asked, true concern heard by the women.

Mary caught the anxious look from Max. The man who usually left the caring for the new ones to others, those who came broken and hurting for the first time to the castle, was not a work he was much involved with, but with this one he seemed truly concerned. Perhaps because he found her, and hopefully in time to help her.

Max left the difficult task of working through the first days to those he thought more qualified, more gifted at cleaning up the hurt. This concern coming from Max today seemed different and sincere. Both Mary and Sophie took notice.

Mary smiled, wondering what went on inside her handsome friends' heart, before she waved her hand in a gentle, dismissal, letting the men know they could leave. Sophie tipped her head and smiled a quizzical smile at Mary, equally puzzled at the reaction from Max.

Now focused on the one in the bed, in a whisper barely heard by others, "You are safe here. My name is Mary Elizabeth, and this is my friend, Sophie." Mary continued, her voice low, "You were carried here by our friend, Max, who found you outside the castle gate. He and his friends brought you inside to us." Mary couldn't be sure the young woman heard, "Sophie and I want to help you if you will let us."

Smiling, Mary asked again as she lifted the broth to her lips, "What is your name?" The weak woman, still not much more than a girl, looked briefly at the beautiful woman holding the cup. Her vision seemed to clear for a moment as she focused on the gentle voice.

The near- frozen maiden finally took a sip, whispering, "Hannah." Taking another sip from the cup Mary held, the girl barely spoke, "My name is Hannah". The eyes dull, her words soft.

Mary caught the soft words, nodded more to herself than others, and leaned close to tuck the soft warm blankets closer around her patient.

Later Sophie held the cup of clear water while Mary lifted the mug of warm broth to the girl's lips a second time. Hannah took small sips at first before seeking more of the warmth. When Hannah finished the broth Mary and Sophie began the work of welcoming this new young one into the castle family by making sure the stranger was warm and comfortable.

Hours later when Hannah opened her eyes and was sufficiently recovered to be taken to a warm room full of steam and a pleasant fragrance, she was bathed and dressed warmly before being taken to a sunroom to rest on an available chaise. Sophie stayed close, giving Mary Elizabeth a hug, "I will stay with Hannah. You go and I will see you later."

Mary turned her head and with a puzzled glance at Sophie, her eyelids bunching, she looked away at nothing. Sophie looked over at the one on the cot, saying, "You and I will see what we can do for this one."

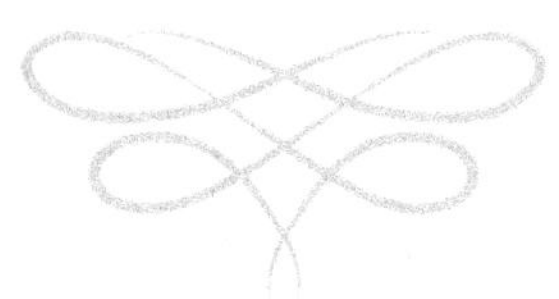

— CHAPTER 3 —

It would not be the first time these two women, (Mary and Sophie), fought together to help someone come out of the dangerous dark, into the castle. Just as someone once helped them in a moment in time to come in from the cold, each one different but each one in her own time, came to this protected haven. They understood each new one held different stories, carried different scars. Each would need all the compassion and help adjusting to a new life in the castle.

Mary looked off at nothing for a moment before looking again at Sophie and smiling, "First, we shall start. We will build a foundation for Hannah. Offer a new way if she is willing."

"Ah, if they are willing. Always if those coming from the dark are willing." Sophie almost laughed.

Mary Elizabeth, older and wiser than Sophie, and the most beautiful person Sophie knew, would weave a safe web around Hannah just as she had when Sophie was new to the castle, carried here by Abba in his coach months ago, shattered and alone. Mary Elizabeth remained close, always there for Sophie from the beginning. Yes, Mary Elizabeth comforted her when there was no one else. Sophie let images, memories flow, and smiled.

Sophie chuckled to herself, "That is the trick! Help them to become willing to change their world. Some can and some struggle to hold onto the dark because it is all they know. It is their 'familiar'."

Mary caught Sophie's gaze and nodded without pointing as she noticed the blood-soaked fabric in a basket to be discarded. "We will do all we can to help this one who calls herself Hanna."

Sophie was glad when the bathing and fresh dressing was finished. The women knew that much of the pain was from Hannah's heart as they tucked her once again into the warm, soft cot. "I will bring her a tray of fruit and stay with her for the afternoon."

Mary smiled and nodded her approval as she left the room and entered a passageway.

$$\text{\scriptsize ❧}\text{——} \quad \textsc{Chapter } 4 \quad \text{——}\text{\scriptsize ❧}$$

Hannah groaned, again calling out, "Joel", after a pause, she whispered, "Joel, I need you", before slipping back into a strange peaceful place. Sophie heard the whisper and wondered who this 'Joel' person was Hannah called for. Someone important to this broken girl. Sophie sat quietly in the bedside chair near Hannah. Hannah slept for several hours while Sophie and others took turns staying nearby and refreshing the water and tea pitchers.

As the sun began to slip out of sight and night drew near Hannah tried to sit up in the narrow bed.

Sophie was quickly at her side to help her, "How do you feel? Are you warm? You were very cold when we found you."

Wrapping her arm around Hannah, Sophie questioned, "Do you have any pain? I am here, I will not leave you. You need only to call out."

Hannah pushed her hair back with trembling fingers, rough from weeks of abuse, and looked at Sophie, "Who are you? Where am I? I don't want to be here. I need Joel, and…….."

Hannah's eyes filled with tears as her voice trailed off into a whisper and she bent her face into her hands.

Ah, how to begin? "My name is Sophie. My husband Henri and I live near the castle. Our friend, Max, found you early this morning by the iron gate against the garden wall. We brought you inside, cared for you, worked to make you comfortable and to do all we can to help you."

"I do not understand." Tears began to slowly trickle down the countenance of the young woman.

Looking at the distraught girl, now warm and clean and rested, Sophie smiled. "Understanding will come. For now, it is enough that you are alive and warm."

Pausing to tuck the quilt in tighter, Sophie said, "You are safe here. This is not a prison, and you may leave anytime you wish. But it is our hope, Abba's and mine and Mary Elizabeth's, that you will stay with us, at least until you regain your strength. Perhaps meet with Abba. This is his castle, and perhaps meet the friend who found you and brought you in out of the cold. His name is Max. He just happened to see a bit of your scarf and your beautiful red hair through the gate."

"Beautiful?" Hannah frowned. "So much red hair is difficult to hide." Hannah gave a slight shrug as she lay back on her pillow and closed her eyes, a tear slipping out, sliding down her cheek.

As tears fell, Hannah spoke softly, "You are right. I am too weak to move much less leave this place." As her eyes closed she murmured, "Thank you for your kindness…….." Her last words barely heard before sleep returned.

Later that first evening, Mary Elizabeth stepped into the room with a fresh pot of hot tea, "How is our newest little one doing?"

"She awoke for a time but has been resting now. Should I try to wake her and get her to come with me? She needs to eat."

Mary smiled at Sophie, "Let her rest. We will bring her warm bread and tea. You will know when it is time for the work of restoration to begin." Mary, eyes closed for a moment, became thoughtful. "The work of rebuilding yet another broken life and filling this one who calls herself Hannah, with true peace is a work worth doing. Knowing she is truly safe here with us is a good beginning. "

Sophie frowned, "She seemed to wake long enough earlier to thank us for our kindness. And she did mention her mother earlier, recognizing the quilt I wrapped in. I think she has family who love her. We must work to find out how we can help."

Mary Elizabeth nodded her agreement, smiling, "A new skein to unravel."

CHAPTER 5

Looking at Sophie, Mary waited, letting Sophie remember her own beginnings here in Abba's castle.

Each new one coming out of the dark, and for some, their first days at the castle could be very different, difficult, and new ones often needed what others could only guess at. Who could know what this one would need? Abba would have the answers.

Sophie opened the heavy drapes to let in the morning sun as she listened to the early sounds of the waking castle.

Just then Henri stuck his head in the doorway of the room, "Hello, my wife, how are things with our newly found person?"

Sophie stood and took the few steps to hug her tall husband and felt him bend to kiss the top of her head. "She is clean and safe, but I think I would like to stay with her, make sure she wakes to see a familiar face. Not sure how long I will be."

"No problem. Stay with her. I will stay with Max and other friends in the East Retreat area." Henri turned for one last glance at his lovely wife, knowing how lucky he was to have found and captured the heart of such a special woman. Lovely, compassionate, and with a heart full of special affection for him, a tall, plain man with little about him most could call special.

Now there was Max, handsome with his dark curly hair and constant smiles, letting those dimples show and charm any one in sight, and not so tall that he had to bend over for a kiss. Henri sighed, thinking 'no matter, I got the girl'. He caught himself smiling as he walked away.

Henri nodded a greeting to Mary Elizabeth as he left. She touched his arm with affection as he passed.

Henri disappeared, barely out of view when Hannah began to toss and moan, "Joel. I need you, Joel. Please, please don't go……" The voice faded into a whisper but not before Sophie watched pain cross the restless girl's brow and tears drift down the side of her gaunt face. So pale, so lost. Sophie knew it would take time and lots of patience and kindness to heal all that was broken in this young woman. How long would it take? All she knew was they would be here for this one called Hannah for as long as she needed them. Each new one folded into the castle life differently. Each one changed and healed differently. Moments, or days, or months, before real transformation could be clearly seen.

As evening closed in, Sophie took a small candle from the hallway and lit several tapers in the wall sconces in Hannah's room to push the darkness out and, taking a quilt, wrapped herself and settled into a large chair by the bedside to wait. Hannah tossed and moaned but did not really come awake until the sunlight began to lighten the eastern horizon, Hannah's third day at the castle. Sophie opened the heavy drapes, doused what was left of the lighted candles and stretched.

As dawn filtered in through the window a strangled cry pierced the dawn, "No, no!!" Hannah tried to get up.

Sophie moved quickly to hold and comfort Hannah, trying to stop the frightened girl's trembling until she was fully awake. "Where am I? Where is Joel?" Slowly, Hannah lay again on the pillows. Her eyes never left Sophies, her questions went unanswered. Sophie did not know the answers.

Hannah kept muttering unintelligible words, but it sounded like she kept saying, "where is she?" Repeatedly mumbled words until she grew silent, and the troubled soul once again fell silent, breathing evenly in sleep.

Darla, Sophie's friend, stepped into relieve Sophie for an hour, with fresh water and a cup of hot herbal tea. Sophie waited until Hannah once again slept before leaving the room, leaving her in Darla's care.

When Sophie returned, she found Hannah awake and sitting on the edge of her cot, drinking tea. Darla had brushed her long tangled red hair and forced it into a loose braid. Hannah, although still oblivious to much of her surroundings, sat in a fresh robe and held the teacup. Sophie gave Darla a quick hug and a wide smile of thanks. She whispered, "Good work."

Darla smiled, "I will stay with you. She is still weak, it will be a pleasure,"

Taking the now empty cup, Sophie asked Hannah, "Are you ready for a short walk? We can go onto the sun porch and have a warm roll and fruit. Not far, just down the passageway. I am a bit hungry. How about you?"

Her eyes still dull and empty, Hannah started to rise. Sophie and Darla helped the weak one out of the room and down a short hallway to a small sunlit room, a few small tables scattered about with two to four individuals at each, having tea and visiting with friends. It felt warm and inviting to the women as they entered. A sideboard holding fresh flowers, bowls of fruit and baskets of warm bread stood along the wall. Dawn was breaking through the windows, sconces along the wall with candles were doused, no longer needed as sunlight filled the room. The three women soaked up the warm peaceful atmosphere.

Sophie settled Hannah at a table with Darla before leaving them to fill plates for all three. Later Darla went for a pot of tea.

Hannah ate a small piece of fruit, then began to eat the warm bread and honey. Sophie and Darla watched, both careful not to let her eat too much or too fast. It was a lovely sunny day and from the inside looking out it was a warm, wonderful morning.

"I am so tired. May I lay down now." Hannah's head began to lower.

"Of course. It is a perfect time for a rest.

Once back in the room, Hannah slept. Sophie opened all the blinds to let the day in and snuggled back into her quilt and chair after she was sure Hannah was comfortably tucked in.

Mary Elizabeth came to spend a moment with Sophie, to see how the night passed, and talk about plans for this new one, who called herself Hannah.

The women whispered, the room held quiet, when Hannah suddenly opened her eyes, looked at Sophie wrapped in the old quilt and smiled. Life seen in the bright green eyes for the first time. "Mama." Mouthing the one word, she smiled and once again slept. Mary looked at Sophie, "She has lost blood but is gaining strength." Mary and Sophie rested their eyes on the sleeping girl.

Mary, her compassion evident on the lovely face let a smile form and then dissolved as she turned to leave the room.

Sophie seemed puzzled at the outcry until Mary uttered on her way out, "It is the quilt. She thought of home and her mother. There must be one similar in her past that carries pleasant memories."

Sophie knew Mary was right. It was the worn but still bright colored quilt causing a familiar image to send the girls memories back to her home and her family. 'Hannah'. Mary was magically gifted at knowing things others could only guess at. Sophie tugged the quilt around her legs for warmth as Mary walked from sight. Sophie snuggled deeper into the heavy chair for comfort, her thought on Mary Elizabeth and this new one called Hannah.

❈⊶——— CHAPTER 6 ———⊷❈

Sophie closed her eyes thinking, Mary always knew how to start the healing process with anyone new to the castle. Always start at the beginning. They would start from when and where Hannah was found, spend time with her, answer questions when one could and help her understand how safe she should feel now that she was in the castle.

Some answers would have to come later. All the healing, both in the heart and the body, and the mind would take time. For some who came into the castle, healing came quickly, in mere moments, for some it took days before progress could be seen, and for others perhaps months or even years. But Abba was here, and the castle always had room for the new ones to come in out of the dark.

Healing would come if one stayed in or near Abba's castle. Stay near those who offered only good to those who sought help. Sophie knew and understood.

Abba found Sophie, near death, brought her home to his castle, where Mary Elizabeth spent many hours and many days with her through her healing process. Now, a very happily married woman with a wonderful husband living in her own cottage near Abba's land, Sophie let excitement bubbly up for the life she now lived and for this new person. The possibilities were endless. Perhaps it was not easy, but there was a wonderful future ahead for Hannah if Sophie had anything to say about it. And, though she did not understand, Hannah was not alone. Abba and Mary Elizabeth and Max, and Darla, and of course, Henri. "Ah, I should think we are off to a good start."

There were things that those at the castle did not, could not know. Days earlier Joel, with a weak and weary Hannah, stumbled onto a deserted stone cabin off the cart track, nearly hidden among a cluster of oak and birch trees. It would soon be dark, and the young man breathed deep, pushed out rising fear and began to do what he could to make Hannah comfortable. He knew she was in pain, along with being exhausted, hungry, and cold. Hannah did not complain but Joel felt her pain. Was it her time?

Joel brought wood for the rock fireplace into the shack, along with fresh fir branches for sleeping pallets. Shaking out the rags and old bedding left behind from earlier occupants, the young man soon felt the warmth fill the hut and watched Hannah as her brow smoothed and she relaxed on the pallet.

He would find food tomorrow; he must find food. He would dig roots, boil bark, do all he could do, set snares for game, he would take care of Hannah. The young man let his head drop. Too little food, too exhausted to think clearly. He needed rest. But rest would have to wait.

The small spring of clear water was closer than he could have hoped. Finding an old bucket and taking his water skin he headed for the trickle of fresh water. Joel knew he needed to rest but rest and food for himself would wait. Now for hot tea for Hannah.

Hannah awoke in the night moaning and then crying out. Joel built up the fire and lit a short piece of saved candle before kneeling beside Hannah. "What is it?"

"It is time." Through tears flowing freely, she clung to Joel's hand, "don't leave me, please never leave me."

Joel settled beside Hannah, tucking the piece of warn blanket and his long coat around her. The fireplace kept most of the cold at bay and the exhausted Hannah slept, before waking from time-to-time moaning, and crying out with pain during the long night.

Joel slept little, waking in darkness to find the fire reduced to embers and Hannah groaning in pain. He stoked the fire, added wood, and tried to soothe her, "I will fetch fresh water and food as soon as it is daylight." He knew about livestock giving birth, but this was his child! It could not be time!

But it was. Joel shook his head trying to clear his scrambled thoughts.

Hannah grabbed his hand, "The wee one is coming."

Joel stood, looking around, seeing nothing, bewildered, "No, it is too soon." Could she be mistaken? He tried to think. They left the village before the turning of the leaves and she knew then, her body held change, normal ways of a woman no longer coming every month. They planned, putting aside things they thought they would need, and left the village before dawn one autumn morning, going before anyone could guess. They knew they would be missed; their parents' plan for their children's futures did not include a grandchild before wedlock. He did not want to shame Hannah, nor cause her to be shunned by their friends and family. So, they slipped quietly away to a future together.

Joel loved Hannah; how could he have led them to this! Here in a cold, nearly empty hovel, with a child coming. Joel knew he was not the man he needed to be. His head hung in total defeat mixed with self-pity, until he remembered their beginning.

Remembering their new love, the raging desire of youth, knowing it was forbidden, Joel and Hannah would find themselves in secluded glens a distance from their village, pushing conscience aside, letting their bodies rule.

Now all those summer days, full of nothing but the thoughts of the two of them together, long since passed, finally brought them here to this cold barren night. Hungry, no family near to help and a little one coming too soon. Joel knew he must get fresh water, boil his knife, be as ready as he could be.

After a long night and the following morning, Hannah gave birth the middle of the afternoon. Once the child was born, Joel stayed busy building the wood supply, gathering plants, setting snares, and getting fresh water. The sassafras tea seemed to calm Hannah. She held the newborn, drank small sips of the offered tea, and ate greens. Joel encouraged her to do all she could to gain strength.

He cut fresh tree bows for bedding, took some of the rags to the stream to wash away signs of the birth, and carried in more than enough wood for the night and the following day, perhaps enough for two nights if they were careful, then he collapsed in the corner on some rags and slept.

Joel felt the exhaustion and fear flow through his soul. What was he going to do? He couldn't wait, he would have to decide what should be done and soon. It was obvious Hannah was not strong enough to travel, Joel was not sure he was. But he must do something, or they would be lost, truly lost. All three of the them.

Hannah drank from the waterskin, but it was not enough to fill her breasts for the babe.

The whimpering of mother and child carried through the long night after the birth. Through the early morning hours Hannah cried as she pleaded with Joel. "Take the babe, get help." Unheard of at first but seeing no other way, he at last agreed, and Joel made his decision. He would do all he could to save his family. Still leaving Hannah even for a day or two seemed impossible ---------. He argued with Hannah.

"No, I cannot leave you. We will stay together." Joel tried to argue even after he realized she was right. Hannah, weak, exhausted but still able to think clearly of the babe, did not relent, she wisely pled for Joel to understand and take their babe to someplace safe before they were all too weak to survive. Though her desire seemed garbled and confused at times, Joel understood. He would do all he could to save their little one.

Joel arose before dawn and prepared. Finally, feeling as ready as possible, he moved to Hannah's pallet to hold her for a moment.

"I will take our babe and find help, then be back for you." Joel hoped to reassure her, "No later than three days. You have water and tea and firewood. I'll be back without fail in three days or less." The young man watched her, hoping she could hear and understood. "Can you do this? Can you stay warm and safe until I return?" She seemed so very tired but forced a small smile. Her eyes seemed distant, empty. Hannah, listless, let the palm of her hand fall open revealing a rosary of small beads. She spoke with her eyes, looking first at the small string of beads, then to Joel, their eyes locking with understanding. Joel tucked the beads into his pocket. Joel understood. A gift for their child from Hannah, her mother, and from Hannah's mother and her mother before.

Hannah seemed disoriented but nodded her approval until she felt the baby being lifted from her. Joel, when he reached for the babe and wrapped Hannah's long scarf around the child, followed by a wool shirt, Hannah cried out once and reached for the child before falling back.

Joel kept the child tucked inside his wool shirt, stepped to the door, and never looked back.

Joel knew they came from a village far to the south and they passed no village near where they were now on this northern cart path, so today he walked a short distance south and turned off the wider, more familiar path, turned west, then with long strides, the young father traveled on foot down a seldom used cart track. Maybe it would lead him to a hamlet or larger village to the west. It was cold, he knew spring could be weeks away and a late snow could cover the land. He must find help or die with the child. The baby, a girl, so quiet, by midday no longer crying. He knew in his heart Hannah gave all she could ever give to save the child. Would she feel the same when her mind cleared? He trudged on, numb but walked steadily west.

Exhausted and ready to surrender to the elements, he kept putting one foot in front of the other until dusk and seemed shocked when he unexpectantly saw a light. Confusion from lack of sleep and exhaustion caused the young man to let his mind wander and considered resting by a tree, let death come for both he and his child. But the young father trudged on, moving one foot in front of the other as the day faded into night.

At first Joel reasoned his eyes played a trick of some kind, the single light in the outlying cottage surly not real. Moving closer, a candlelight could be seen through the window of the hut, then he spotted a second dwelling with a light farther down the lane.

Must be a small hamlet. Putting one foot in front of the other he reached the first front door he came to. He thought to knock but felt confused, tried to think, when the door quietly opened before him.

A small girl, perhaps six, said, "We heard you on the stoop. Who are you?" turning to her mother she said, "It is a strange man." The woman of the house came closer, noticed the dazed man, saw that his hands lifted something toward her. He held something small. Without speaking, she gathered the bundle to her chest. Looking into the eyes of the man only once, she carried the bundle the few steps to settle into a chair by the hearth. Tears glistened as she lowered herself into the wicker chair, slowly unbuttoned her blouse and placed the nearly frozen child to her aching breasts. Tears continued to move slowly down her cheek as the mother encouraged the little one to suckle.

"Tilly, give the man who brought this miracle to us a bowl of stew and hot tea." Tilly, though small, rushed to do her mother's bidding. Once the stew was served, Tilly moved closer to the fire, where she stood by her mother's chair. The mother and daughter seemed overwhelmed, both smiling through tears, unable to take their eyes off the baby. A true miracle!

42

CHAPTER 7

Joel finished the stew and closed his eyes, his head drooped.

"Tilly, (probably short for Matilda), take the man to the corner there and settle him on the cot."

"Yes, mama." Joel did not resist as the girl took his hand and guided him to the pallet where he lay down and was soon asleep.

Dawn broke the following morning with the mother sitting in the chair by the hearth, as though she hadn't moved. Joel watched her from where he lay, filled with wonder. Had she been at the hearth all night? The woman smiled as her gaze held on the little one, now latching for more. Joel heard the woman whisper, "She is purely a gift from God."

Joel wondered how that could be. He and the babe had nearly frozen, starved, and, in truth, should be dead. But here they were. He, warm and rested and the baby is alive and nursing. The smiling woman looked at the baby as a miracle. Joel could not argue. It truly seemed a miracle.

Joel arose, nodded to the woman, and went out to relieve himself and bring in more wood. When he returned with loaded arms, the woman, her lips turned up slightly, nodded to the young man. "There is porridge on the rod iron. Please help yourself."

"Thank you." Joel carried a bowl to the hearth and filled it. The woman remained silent and watched him eat. The little girl, Tilly, came from behind a curtain, sleeping quarters he supposed, and walked to stand by her mother. With tousled hair, and pushing sleep from her eyes, the youngster stood near her mother's chair and smiled down at the now sleeping child before lifting her gaze to meet his. The small girl in her crumpled night dress and loosened tangled braids, her eyes filled with questions, held her gaze on the man, her look of wonder filled her countenance before she smiled at Joel. He knew he would forever carry the image of that smile with him. A beautiful memory to hold close.

Joel did not feel like a man who just delivered a miracle to this small house. He thought of Hannah. He ached for her. His decision made; Joel worked to pay the woman back for her kindness to him and his daughter. He cut and carried wood inside for the hearth and stacked more wood outside of the door. He carried fresh water and filled the buckets and large containers; all he could find. When he finished, he spoke to the woman, asking her if there was anything else he could do for her. He held his cloth hat, crumpled, in his hands as he spoke with her. She looked squarely at Joel, "I thank you for all you have done for me and Tilly. And the gift of the babe to replace one lost will forever be a miracle to me."

Joel not sure how to respond, told the woman he must go. He was needed elsewhere.

She understood but concern crossed her countenance. Laying the infant in a crib made for another, she turned to Joel, tears of gratitude threatening. "You have worked all day this day, so please stay, rest tonight and leave refreshed at first light."

Joel knew he would be stronger from food and another night's rest, and he could spend another night near his daughter, so he agreed.   As Joel walked from the warm home the following morning, he looked back to see Tilly standing by her mother, waving a small hand.

Earlier the woman prepared a satchel of food for Joel, and he filled his water skin with fresh water. He turned only once to etch the outline of the cottage in his memory before turning back to the path where he picked up his pace. He felt grateful for a fair day and a full belly. He would reach Hannah much quicker now that he was rested and fed.

Emptiness filled Joel, not having the small one to hold. But the emptiness moved over for a bit of joy that settled in his bones knowing his daughter was truly safe.

His thoughts pitched in all directions. Joel remembered telling Hannah to wait three days. This was his third day away from her. Would she be there? It had taken a few hours longer than expected to regain strength and do choirs to repay the woman and her child for saving his life. And the life of his child. Would Hannah understand there was no other choice? And still it was only the third day. He would make things right. He would be there with her soon. Thinking as he followed the track east, he wondered. So weak after giving birth, he could not rid himself of the fear he would find her dead. He walked until he was exhausted, rested until he feared falling asleep and ate a small portion of food in the bag before continuing east, finally reaching the wider track and turning north.

Much of the path did not look familiar until he found the northern trail. Once he made the turn, he knew the shack and Hannah must be nearby. When he saw the cabin, agony filled him. No smoke could be seen coming from the chimney. Joel began to jog, fear choking him, "Please let her be alive!" he opened the sagging door slowly, feeling the cold emptiness even before he stepped in.

The shack was empty, Hannah gone. The ashes in the hearth were cold. Most of the wood he'd left was burned and some of the water, but no Hannah. Joel, after realizing he was too late and filled with fear, he felt bile fill his throat. Could she have left, tried to follow him in her weakened, confused condition?

"Hannah, Hannah," Joel whispered then began to call her name loudly as he ran in all directions from the hut searching for some sign, "Where are you, Hannah?"

Finally close to collapse, Joel slumped to the ground not far from the hut, "She is dead. No sign of how she died, something or someone must have carried her off." After he sat in misery for long moments, Joel lifted his eyes and looked around where he sat. He lifted his head to gaze at the woods around the hut. His search turned up nothing, no sign of Hannah but Joel felt her. "She is alive. I would know if she were dead."

As dusk enveloped the land and early stars in the northern sky could be seen, the young man stood, wiped tears from his eyes, "'I'll widen the search tomorrow. As more evening stars appeared, he gathered wood for a fire in the stone hearth. "I will stay the night and continue tomorrow. There must be something I missed." Adding wood to the fire, he prepared for the night.

Grief laid on him, so heavy he could not stand. He settled on the crude pallet knowing he failed to protect her, to take care of the woman he loved. He should have stayed with her. At that moment the realization settled on the young man; he deeply loved and needed Hannah more than any could imagine. Joel felt his failure, much like a sharp knife wound.

Joel lay curled on the pallet and wept until there were no more tears, until only a deep agonizing emptiness filled him. He knew his child lived and he felt Hannah still lived and would do all in her power to live for the child and for him. It was only a feeling, but the young man hung tightly to the feeling.

Joel stayed on the pallet through the night, rising from time to time to feed the fire. He could not rest knowing this was the very place he left Hannah, where he last held her, where he lifted their child and carried the tiny infant away. A child another woman now nourished, Hannah's baby, their daughter. Would Hannah approve, or hate him for taking her baby from her? It was Hannah's wish, but would she remember and grow to despise him. Joel felt tears well, having no answer.

On the very pallet where he left Hannah only four days ago, Joel decided he could not live. The loss, his failure from the very beginning choked him. How could so much go wrong so quickly? Joel felt sick. He crawled to the door and out onto the ground, where he continued to lay, sick until there was nothing left, until he felt numb with despair.

The night grew cold with blasts of wind coming from nowhere.

The cold night wind forced Joel back into the hut. Still too weak to add wood to the fire, he once again lay curled on the pallet, tried to feel something anything, perhaps even something intangible, left behind by Hannah, and finally admitting defeat, the lover, the father, the young man wrapped in hopelessness, slept.

CHAPTER 8

Months now passed since Joel left his home without a backward glance, full of excitement and plans for a future with Hannah. At first, he found jobs, provided a place to rest and food to fill their bellies, but once the last of the fields were harvested and the garden vegetables placed in cellars to feed families through the winter, work became scarce. So, with the winter now nearly upon them, even the work helping to slaughter and prepare smoke houses for curing the hams and meat were finished. The winter fell hard. They continued north, Hannah growing heavy with child. Eating off the land and finding shelter each night became more and more difficult. Most hamlets they did encounter were hesitant to become involved with strangers.

Joel needed work and a place to keep Hannah safe, but for three days they passed no villages, found no work. They were running out of food. The last of the wild berries were gone, snow covered much of the ground, at time the cart route hard to follow.

It was growing daily closer to time for the baby to be born and now each day brought regrets and unbearable grief where there used to be joy. Hannah grew weaker as they followed the early stars and moved north. The couple traveled less each day until finally they came upon the small stone cottage. The hut was empty so they would stay here for now, a decision made by Joel, Hannah simply too weak to care.

Joel lay in the dark, considering. The past few days were a blur. Now back at the stone hut and finding no Hannah, Joel knew he could still go home. He could go, fetch his daughter and go home. Home. A place he once eagerly ran from, with Hannah holding tightly to his hand .

Ah, Hannah! Joel shook his head, his chest feeling tight. Thoughts tumbled across his mind. Hannah gone, probably dead. He meant to get back in time, care for her. But nothing worked in his, in their favor. One right thing, the baby was safe and warm with the woman and her daughter Tilly.

Joel slept, he dreamed of home, his mother opening the door, reaching to touch him. He dreamed of the joy the baby would bring to his usually stoic mother, her smile, her tender way of holding the child. Yes, he could go home after getting his daughter from the dear woman who saved her life.

But could he? The babe even now was less than a week old. He knew his home was miles to the south. Did he dare try such a journey with a small infant? Would the villagers accept him? Winter weather turned warm as spring approached, but cold wind still blew daily.

And what of Hannah's family? He and the child would surely be shunned, perhaps even by his own mother.

In his dream, Joel saw his mother smile. Her son, the young man, so like his father, her affection so evident toward her child, now grown.

Joel awoke rested and warm after hours of sleep and stretched before he remembered. Shame came over him, a heavy blanket of remorse weighed him. Taking the infant and leaving Hannah was the only thing he could do, wasn't it? She was too weak to travel, and it had taken all his strength to survive and find food for the baby. A miracle really! Still, he promised Hannah he would return in three days if not sooner with food. He knew she trusted him. But Hannah left or was taken. Gone without a trace. Where could she get the strength to leave? Did she try to follow him?

After leaving the child, he returned. But even though it was the eve of the third day, Joel realized he was too late. Too late! For whatever reason, she left. The young father decided to search, really search for Hannah, for some trace in the cabin or the area around the cabin. Joel gathered wood and water from the creek and straightened the cabin each morning before making ever bigger circles around the area in search of a clue, looking for anything out of the ordinary. The babe was safe and too young for him to take away from the wetnurse, from Tilly's ma. He would go fetch his daughter but first he would make every effort to find Hannah or a trace, a clue that could help him.

Days passed. A week later, after an unexpected late winter snowfall, Joel admitted defeat. Hannah did not return, and he found no sign of her ever having been in or around the hut. There was nothing to hold him here.

Once he realized Hannah was lost to him, Joel prepared to travel to get his daughter. He laid traps for rabbits and small game, smoked the meat, gathered the last of greens, nuts, and roots still to be found in the area. A few days later, he felt ready, as ready as he would ever be. He would go west to where he left his child, take his daughter home to his mother. He refused to think about the long trip with the newborn. Doubts came but he pushed them out. Thoughts filled his mind. Perhaps he should take his time. Afterall, it was the waning months of winter. The world would soon be greeting the warmer months of spring. He would try to find work and give himself time to heal from the loss of Hannah before he headed home. Perhaps give the babe time to wean.

Finally, he decided to wait, give him and his daughter time to heal, time to bond.

Decisions made, he would take his time, make sure his thinking was clear this time. Winter was leaving as the first sprouts of Spring arrived. Joel began to feel more normal with less pain and better sleep. He prepared, and finally one clear morning he headed down the wide cart track to the narrow track leading west. He knew he felt much stronger than on that long first march to save his child. What a long day into a cold night that trip had been!

After walking several hours, seeing the sun high, Joel thought of finding a place to stop and have his noon meal. Walking around a gentle curve in the track Joel was surprised to see another person on the road. Well, not exactly on the track, more settled on the side of the cart path, sitting with his hand on the handle of a cart full of wood. The man looked to be very old, quite wizened. As Joel approached, the old man drew back until Joel offered a drink from his waterskin. The old man took a drink, re-corked the water jug and handed it back to Joel, who by now was seated beside him. Joel offered him a piece of dried fish which the old man accepted and both men leaned back to relax as Joel said, "You are the first person I have seen all day. What brings you here?" Adding, "you look like you could use a bit of help with the cart".

Looking directly at Joel, the old man said, "Could be you came along at just the right time." He chuckled as he pushed back his cloth hat and scratched his brow first, then his beard, "I sat down because I gave out. Need to get this home to the woman or I'll have no supper but be danged if I can get up much less pull the wood on home." Stopping for a moment, "By the way, my name is John Peterson. Just call me John."

Joel extended his hand, "I'm called Joel."

Mr. Peterson reminded Joel of his father, or who his father might have been had he lived. A man always willing to trek out into the cold to help anyone in need.

Perhaps the kind of man Joel hoped he could be. Joel and the old man talked, shared stories as they both chewed on strips of dried fish and rested.

Mr. Peterson shared his and his wife's story, "We never cared about the easy life, work makes a body feel good, at least that's the way I think."

Finally, as the minutes passed, Joel said, "We should get you on home." He helped the old man to his feet, "Just point the way and me and the cart will follow."

"It's not a far piece." The old man stood to his feet with the help of a long staff.

Joel followed the slow progress of the old man, finally reaching a cottage with smoke coming out of the chimney and a stout woman wearing a long apron standing in the doorway, "Well, I see you bring company." She smiled at Joel, "Grateful I am that you brought the old soul home. I tell him we'll send for one of the boys, but he is as stubborn as they come."

Joel looked around the cozy room, before he asked, "Do you have family?"

The woman smiled as the old man spoke of two sons, no longer making their homes nearby.

"I miss them, but not like Mrs. She has some drawings, likenesses of both sons, one thing the old girl treasures. Still, we are content, but you came along at a good time. Blessing us with getting the wood in so we have more than enough to get us through. A blessing for sure."

"Glad, I am to be of service and your woman is a good cook." Joel chuckled thinking of the roast and vegetables from the root cellar he devoured at their noon meal.

The old man stood silent for a time, "and you, do you have a family?"

Joel felt odd not knowing how to answer, finally admitting he was going to fetch his daughter.

"And your woman?"

Joel did not answer. John was thoughtful, "Where will you take the wee one when you get her?" The woman seemed troubled by talk of the little one.

Joel stopped, sat down, and told the kind folks all of it. So much sadness.

"You have a sad tale, and it brings you much pain to tell it. I just say from my heart what I know, you hang on and things will come right." For some unknown reason Joel believed the old man.

The old man seemed so confidant with his words. Joel stood, picked up his sack and waterskin and said, "Thank you for listening." There was nothing else to say.

After the filling meal with the old couple, and the time past midday, Joel prepared to leave. John told Joel the village he sought could be reached in a couple of hours. He shared the names of friends he and his wife knew there and told Joel if he decided to stay in the village for a time, his friend who ran a forge and blacksmith shed, could maybe use a hand. Joel knew it was time to go get his daughter, still he knew he would remember John and his dear wife. And the name of John's friend, Piper, at the forge. Yes, he would remember John and the name of John's friend.

As the young man walked toward the village, his thoughts flowed to Hannah. Remembering their times together in the wooded areas while still so innocent. The afternoon passed quickly.

CHAPTER 9

The morning sun rose over the castle as Mary and Sophie moved Hannah to a larger room, giving her an armoire for her clothing and a pitcher and bowl for fresh water. The process of filling the needs of a new one to the castle was familiar to Sophie. Remembering, she received much the same care herself in the beginning, her first few hours here in this place; the first truly safe place in her existence.

Some can and will accept change more quickly than others. How long it would take for this new one called Hannah, no one knew.

Mary always advised each one to begin at the beginning, So Sophie walked with Hannah in the mornings before tea, talking, encouraging, sharing and later in the day when she could they would set and watch the day end with the sunset. Hannah was listless and often wanted to be left alone in her room once parted from Sophie.

"I am grateful to you, for all you've done. For saving my life and caring for me but I just want to be alone, to sleep." Sophie listened and waited, each day hoping for positive change.

Mary often joined Sophie and Hannah at meals or later for walks in the gardens. The two friends would talk often of new ways to encourage and help Hannah. If they only knew more about her past, perhaps they would know what to do. Each person came to the castle with different needs, different hurts hard to describe, or some came with darkness in their soul. The important part of any healing mission is to get the broken one to talk, to share their pain. Shared pain is always easier to handle under the umbrella of many seeking healing for their selves while seeking healing for others.

If only they could help Hannah, bring her out of herself into a healthy new way. Abba encouraged Hannah's new friends to simply accept her, to gently care for her and learn to love her. And be patient.

After being with them in the castle for a fortnight, Hannah began to take longer walks, usually alone or with Sophie, often letting tears fall. Such sadness was hard to witness, even though Sophie tried to understand. She knew there were many kinds of pain, and some she was forced to admit were unfamiliar to her.

It was not so very many months ago that Sophie was found by Abba, brought out of the dark on a truly wretched night, brought to the castle in his magical coach. Brought to the castle to heal, find purpose, fall in love with Henri, and have the life offered them here in the castle. Now married her life was indeed full. How could she hope to understand Hannah while having such a good life and knowing Hannah still felt as though she had nothing to live for? Ah, though nearly forgotten, Sophie could remember much of her own past. She would have faith for her new friend,

Sophie smiled as she and Hannah now sat on the same stone bench in the garden that she and Mary Elizabeth sat on so many months ago on Sophie's first full day here in the garden, warm and dry, but still so full of fear and anger on the inside. Mary was very patient with Sophie and now Sophie would be very patient with Hannah. Change can be a slow process but need not be if one will get out of the way and let healing begin.

"Are you warm enough?" The April winds and dark clouds brought back the feeling of winter. Sophie bent to touch Hannah, to make sure she was bundled against the weather. It was Hannah's forth week in the castle and still the girl rarely spoke more than a word or two and only then if spoken to. Mary and Sophie both spoke to Abba, the king of the castle, for advice on what they should do. He let his hand rest on each of their heads and smiled, "You will know when Hannah lets you know." Abba looked away before saying, "For now, just keep doing what you are doing. The time for healing and peace comes differently to each one who joins us here."

Sophie wanted to understand and help this new one, but also wanted to see progress. A breakthrough for Hannah. Something to prove she and Mary were on the right path. But Hannah seemed locked in the past in a way that Sophie could not understand. Sophie remembered the morning Max found her nearly frozen to death and carried her into the castle where she now lived among people who truly cared for her. Now clean and well fed and dressed much like the others, she looked much like the others except for the veil of sadness that hovered over her much of the time.

Mary Elizabeth saw things others could not see and knew more than she spoke of from the first hours with Hannah. Mary kept these insights locked inside. She would know when to share, if ever.

Sophie understood her friend Mary, with her special way of knowing things, and Sophie knew she would help to make the new one comfortable, without knowing the cause of Hannahs secret pain.

Still there was something in the girl's past, a piece of her heart somehow shattered into fragments causing a sorrow so deep that it cast a shadow over her countenance much of the time. Sophie felt a new determination to help, to find a way for the healing to begin.

On one of their walks together, Sophie asked, "Do you feel safe here, Hannah?"

A puzzled look crossed Hannah's brow before she said, "Yes. I think I do." Lowering her head of tousled red hair, she continued softly, "Most of the time I feel nothing, nothing at all, but I am clean and warm and yes, I feel safe here."

Sophie remained silent, waiting.

Finally, Hannah turned to Sophie, "I need to find Joel. I need him."

Ah, a crack. Not really a breakthrough but a small opening.

"You spoke of Joel when we first found you. Henri and Max went out to look for him, the one you call Joel. They went quite far; and they believe they eventually found the small shack you spoke of while you were still most ill. The place was cold and empty, no sign of anyone having been there recently. They spent several days out looking around the area. They met a few folks, but no one remembered meeting anyone by the name of Joel. They tried but found no trace." Hoping to put the girl at ease, Sophie asked, "Is Joel a child? Is he family?" Sophie did not mention the traces of blood found when Hannah first arrived.

"Joel and I were together. Meant to be together forever." Gasping, Hannah whispered "I must leave." The words came in an anguished cry, barely discernable to Sophie.

Sophie was startled by the force of the statement. "Truly, they searched for your friend.

They would tell you if there was even a trace, some clue to follow. There was nothing."

Sophie waited, took a deep breath, holding in the air, sensing a breakthrough. Hannah continued to pause, looking at the early blooms of beauty around her, trying to relax and enjoy the garden. Not wanting to say the wrong thing, Sophie remained silent, waited, and smiled at the girl with the mass of red hair, now mostly tucked under the hood of her cloak.

Hannah finally turned to look at Sophie, "I need to go home. I think Joel has gone home to his mother. You have said this is not a prison, I may go when I wish. So will you help me?"

"Where is the village? How far did you come before you found the castle?" Sophie felt a surge of hope, but Hannah, with head bent into her hands began to weep.

"Hannah, we can help you. Please let us. First, we will plan for you to go home as soon as we know you are strong enough to make the trip. We must find where you are from. We will go with you when the time is right, perhaps later this summer. There may be a smaller castle along the way where we could rest before we reach your village. It is best to talk to Abba and search for the right way forward. Did you come from the north?"

Hannah dipped her chin, tears fell, "No, I remember Joel always talking of going north, so our village must be to the south." She paused, trying to remember, "We must have started somewhere in the south. Joel said he was guided by the stars, but there were few villages found along the paths we took. Joel found little work and soon our food supply was gone. Finally, I became too weak to travel further."

Sophie felt the young woman's pain. There must be a way to help her heal. Abba's home and those who lived and worked here, would do all in their power to see her well and healthy.

That evening at home in their cottage, Sophie asked Henri for his thoughts on how to help Hannah. Henri, always a reasoned thinker, said, "She reminds me in many ways of you when Abba first brought you in from the dark. But there is something we do not know about this one. I believe there is something she has hidden in her heart. Something that brings so much pain she refuses to let any part of herself think of it. Hannah spoke of someone called Joel. She has indicated to you and, at other times, to Mary Elizabeth that Joel is a young man. Her young man. But she is holding back something. Something............"

"I know. But what and how do I, we, gain her trust? And what of Max? He is so taken with Hannah he can hardly keep his eyes off her. This has been true since the first morning he found her."

"Ah, Max imagines himself in love, mostly because he knows Hannah is still thinking of that fellow Joel."

"You don't believe he is serious?"

"Oh, he is as serious as Max can be as long as the girl's heart turns toward another." Henri chuckled, "I am not sure Max will ever settle down. Hannah may prove me wrong. But I know my friend Max quite well."

Sophie laughed, "Well, if any one does you do."

The following day, Sophie took Hannah to the library, a large room with shelves on three sides and tall windows on the east wall. There were hundreds of books and manuals. This room brought more joy to Sophie, especially in the beginning, here in Abba's castle than any other. She hoped Hannah would feel the same joy today. "Do you enjoy reading?"

Hannah looked around, amazed at what she saw. She turned to look at Sophie, a puzzled look, creases on her brow, "Do you read?"

Sophie smiled, understanding the girl's confused expression. "Yes, I read. And since being here, I have the good fortune of coming often to this room to read anything I desire until my eyes grow tired. Would you like to learn to read?"

"Are you sure it is permitted?" Hannah looked shocked and withdrew, as though from some unnamed fear.

Sophie led Hannah to a small table by one of the long narrow windows. Once seated she said, "Yes, here it is permitted." Sophie knew much of the country did not permit learning to read but she enjoyed reading and here in the castle it was permitted. She smiled at Hannah, "I will get a book and we can begin today if you like."

Ah, an opening. A place for a new beginning. Sophie smiled, "Yes, I must say it is my favorite room in all the castle. I know in many places it is forbidden but here, in Abba's castle, I can read until my eyes grow tired. Perhaps it will relieve your mind. Reading calms me and there are so many books,"

"What good will it do? Will it bring Joel back, will it bring back all that I have lost?" Tears threatened.

Sophie looked away before saying, "How will we know if we do not try. Change often brings new ways of looking at life." She glanced at Hannah and then looked down, before she continued with confidence, "I can teach you to read. What do you think? Shall we try?"

Sophie went to a nearby shelf and pulled a slender volume. When Sophie opened the book full of colorful pictures and big words Hannah's expression changed from dour to genuine delight.

For the first time in days, there was light in Hannah's eyes not seen there before. A shift, evident to no one except Sophie, an unexpected but cheerfully accepted gift. Sophie remembered her first days in the castle, her fears, and the feeling of being nothing, so unworthy, before her first day in the library.

Mary Elizabeth opened this wonderful new world to the broken girl, to Sophie, not long out of the dark. And today Sophie could do the same for Hannah. Sophie smiled, to no one in particular, thinking about the night Abba found her near death at the base of a lamp post in a seaport hamlet, and carried her here to his castle in his mystical carriage that floated above the ground. Impossible, but today, here with Hannah and hundreds of books, Sophie could have laughed knowing nothing is impossible. Nothing!

As days passed one by one into spring and turned toward summer, Hannah learned to read. She and Sophie spent hours in the library, moving from early primers to books on gardening, geography, even romance. Hannah smiled often and Max seemed totally smitten by the lovely young woman when he encountered her, but a sadness could still be felt at times when her countenance shifted into a place hidden to the rest of the world. A broken place still refusing to heal. Sophie spoke to Abba about not knowing what to do. She wanted desperately to make things better for Hannah.

Abba's gentle clear voice instructed, "Her truth will be told in time. Stay with her as often as you notice her alone. I see you blessing her daily, just keep up what you are doing."

Sophie knew Abba was right, he always knew when and how healing would come. In the evening she spoke to Henri about her time with Abba. "I trust Abba and will be patient."

Henri nodded, a slight expression of concern, "And now how do you feel? I would like my wife to be more at peace with her new friend." With that said, Henri pulled his wife onto his lap, "I think Abba sees beyond what we can even imagine, and he will help Hannah find peace."

CHAPTER 10

Hannah tossed in her cot as she dreamed restless dreams of love, and loss, and hunger, and youthful desire and the longing for more freedom. She and Joel were adults, or so they believed. Without asking for counsel, unable and unwilling to wait, they planned as well as they could, taking what they could carry and slipped quietly from the village. Feeling free out in the unknown, in the beginning both remembered some fear and trepidation early into their trip, after leaving their village, their homes. Both Hannah and Joel ignored the warning signs.

Joel had what he wanted, a lovely girl to meet all his needs, she wanted nothing in return except his love and protection. That is all Hannah ever spoke of. Oh, Hannah never spoke of it, but Joel knew she felt his failure. She must.

Though never speaking of it, he knew on a deep level that he failed. Joel realized how Hannah must have known he was not man enough to take care of her. In a few short months he left her weak and sick, to die alone in a drafty shack far from home. A far distance from her mother and safety. His youth and lack of experience came wafting in through the dark, bringing deep shame. Only in his bed in the darkness, could he face the fact that he was a coward. Just a boy, not a man! Was it too late? Ah, of course it was too late. Joel knew Hannah was gone.

Joel ran over all of it in his mind. He could not go home. It was too late, or was it? Joel wept into his pillow.

Though young, Joel was older than Hannah by a few months, still younger than many of the village men. His hair was light brown, straight and too long to stay in place unless oiled or wet, and fell over his wide spaced brown eyes much of the time. His skin was clear and tanned from being out in all kinds of weather. This was true even before he and Hannah ran from the village months ago. Hannah often called him handsome. He knew that was just the way she saw him through love-filled eyes.

After his father's death Joel felt a responsibility for his mother and the land. But he and Hannah both longed to see more of life before they were forever anchored in this small village, to their families and to the small piece of land. So, with very little thought of others, they slipped away to live together.

Now the nights were long and full of pain. How long would he suffer for his mistakes? Was loving Hannah wrong? No, not wrong just wrong timing,

Joel remembered the first time he noticed Hannah. Closing his eyes, he recaptured the image. She must have been thirteen or fourteen at the time and her wild red hair full of curls could not be contained under her snood. Even with a scarf knotted in back at the nape of her neck, the hair gradually forced its way out to spring in small curls around her neck and face. Of course, Joel could not approach her, but their eyes met from time to time. Over the following months they watched for a glimpse of each other and would deliberately meet when one or the other could slip away, until finally they found themselves away, hidden in the woods, together. His emotions raged out of control. Joel knew this was love – what else could it be? Hannah and Joel lay on the bed of soft grass and ferns and let emotions carry them to places previously unknown.

Their hearts and bodies took them to forbidden places. On the peripheral edge of thought, they knew they had gone too far, there was no going back to the quiet summer days filled with the work of getting into the garden and later, gathering and storing food for the winter. Things would never be the same.

Joel smiled into the darkness. What could it be? The feelings were new, secret and wonderful. The two of them could not undo what happened even if they wanted to. They would be exposed and punished, both realized the danger and were fearful of some in the village. They tried to let it go, to feel nothing, to stay away, out of the presence of each other, but their longing was impossible to deny, so they finally spent stolen time to gather, made plans to find new lives far away, someplace safe, and left their village under a harvest moon.

To leave all they knew behind and try to find a new place where they could be together felt like an exciting new adventure, a new life to the young people. They could hardly wait for Joel to be sure his mother's wood supply would hold her warm through the cold months of the coming winter and the vegetables were gathered and placed safely in the dugout cellar. Once Joel felt satisfied his mother would not suffer in his absence, Joel felt ready to leave, start a new life with Hannah. The lovers knew Hannah was with child so they would leave and start a new life together. Joel and Hannah could hardly remain normal and contain their excitement the last few days in the village. Finally, it was time, the moon was full, they would head north and see where the stars led them. Such relief and joy as they left their village, their homes, their parents behind! Hannah laughed at everything and nothing as Joel talked of finding work and making their way to a new life.

Thinking back, Joel knew there were other ways. They could have asked permission, posted bans, and waited. Others suffered the waiting, the separation. Why didn't he? Why didn't they talk? Hannah would have done anything he wanted.

Things began to unravel soon after they left. Even though they felt their plan had merit, they ran out of food in less than a week and found it hard to rest or sleep out in the cold nights. It was late fall, soon the snow would come, then what? Joel sought a place to shelter but villages were miles apart and in those they passed through they found doors locked against intruders at dusk. Just like home. Ah, home!

Joel stole a blanket from outside a small dwelling one night. The blanket helped keep Hannah warm. He tried to find fresh water every day, and most of the time was successful. Wells and streams were available much of the time.

Still, he felt lost, and Hannah seemed paler and weaker by the day. He knew he must find food and shelter soon. He could not think how far they traveled, all he knew was that he marked North by the stars every night and followed in that direction every day. Work was now difficult to find, and their progress slow, but he plodded north, encouraging Hannah. She was ill, he must find safe shelter soon.

"I believe there are villages to the north! There must be." He could not cover his frustration.

They traveled northward and finally found the abandoned stone hut. The building was nothing more than a shack, isolated and uninhabited, and seemed abandoned, for months, perhaps for years. He found few things of any use inside except for a bent kettle and a small fireplace. There were a few rags stacked and piled in one corner. A place to rest, perhaps stay warm and sheltered. The hut, even in its lowly condition, was appreciated. Joel gathered twigs and sticks and started a fire with his flint. The young man was thankful. They would survive. Joel built a small fire and brought in fir branches for a pallet for Hannah. He took the rags outside for a good shake. She could finally rest out of the weather. Then he went in search of food and water.

Joel searched and found a small bucket with a handle. Rusty but he was hopeful it would hold water - if he found any. He carried the kettle and bucket in search of water. Near dusk he staggered onto a small creek he almost missed in the shadows. The small spring trickled, and Joel slowly filled the containers and gathered watercress before he started back the way he came. He found Hannah asleep in the still warm cabin and heated the kettle for a bit of tea, the last of their supply. He poured the tea carefully into their tin cups before waking Hannah. He saved the rest of the water to wash in.

Things would look better in the morning. They ate the watercress. As darkness fell, Joel lay beside Hannah who smiled and thanked him for taking care of them.

The next day things slowly grew untenable. Hannah struggled in pain through the day into the night, and finally near dawn a child was born. Hannah pled, when she seemed coherent, for Joel to save their child.

She pleaded with him to go, find help. Joel realized Hannah was right, he knew he must leave to save the child, their child. The baby was swaddled next to Hannah and Joel realized Hannah seemed confused, barely realized the child was with her. Hannah was too weak to travel.

Joel considered every possibility and finally made the difficult decision to go for help while he still had enough strength. He promised Hannah he would return in three days. No more than three. He left enough water and what food he could forage before embracing her one last time. Lifting the infant into his coat and holding fast, he gathered his water skin and left the small stone shack.

Joel never looked back. He knew if he was to live, if they were to live, he must get help. But the country was unfamiliar. Later when he came to a track heading west, he turned hoping for help before he and the newborn died.

CHAPTER 11

The last of the winter snow covered much of the ground around the castle and the winds blew cold. Days moved on, each one as miserable as the last for all those living lives outside of the castle. Through these days, with the spring months looming, but slow to appear, Hannah spent hours in the library and learned to read. First children's books with drawings, then books with only words. For the first time since her arrival here in Abba's world, Hanna's green eyes sparkled with a measure of joy. She rarely mentioned Joel. Some mornings she awoke with a sob, her face pressed against a damp pillow but as dawn broke, with good food, friends, and more books than she could ever dream of, she changed, her countenance held peace. Her days were full. She enjoyed sharing tasks with

Mary Elizabeth and of course, with Sophie and the others who, overtime, became friends.

At different intervals, Max and Hannah could be seen at tea, conversing about books she recently read, Max helping her with difficult words and phrases. They often could be seen laughing at phrases in her latest book or laughing at nothing at all. An unnamed sadness could be seen covering Hannah much like a dark mist now and then but not as evident as it had been just a few short weeks ago. The red-haired girl began to glow with good health and a level of joy covered her as she let the darkness slip from her countenance during the day. The nights were different.

Sophie, along with Henri and Mary Elizabeth watched and waited for her to share with them what troubled her nights, but Hannah did not offer anything. They were determined to speak with Abba. And wait. All in good time, no need to force.

Hannah began to help with the children, spending hours every day with some of the younger ones. Slowly she was much changed. Not healed from some hidden brokenness, but able to smile, even laugh with the children at times. There seemed to be an invisible bond between her and the small children.

Perhaps the only one who suspected her secret was Mary Elizabeth. Too soon after the birth of a child, too much evidence, the swollen breast, excessive bleeding when carried to the castle her first day. Yes, there had been a birth, Mary seemed sure of that, but what happened to the child. And where was the man, Joel? Mary Elizabeth talked to Abba about ways to reach Hannah, help her to get past her memories.

Abba encouraged with a small smile, only saying, "All in good time. Things will come right."

All Mary Elizabeth could do was trust Abba, encourage Hannah, and believe. Much like Abba, she felt and knew things others could not fathom. She would wait and do all within her power to help Hannah start a new and different life. Mary knew this could be a slow process, still she and others were much encouraged by the changes already evident. Hannah would live and find peace here in the castle, they were sure of it.

The only problem Mary could see was Max and his feelings for the redheaded girl. Max always flirted harmlessly with one and all, but this relationship felt different to Mary. Max was, or at least thought he was, in love with Hannah. Was he or did he know without knowing he knew that she belonged to someone else? Max gathered much of his strength from his friend, Henri Cabot. Was he strong enough to survive a broken heart? Max always seemed drawn to the shiny object he could not reach.

Perhaps this is another such heart experience for Max. Mary Elizabeth knew her friend sheltered himself with an internal lock from getting hurt and he did not think of his flirting as hurtful. Some could be hurt but Max knew he only intended to enjoy flirting to pleasantly pass the time. Sophie knew there would come a time when the tables turned, perhaps this would be that time. Mary and Sophie discussed Max. Sophie knew Henri would be there for his friend, to help him through any real or imagined hurt, back to a happy life. Storms are scary when you are going through one, but eventually the sun always shines again. And difficult times were always better with a friend. Perhaps Max will become more aware of the dangers that come with bad, (even if it is fun), behavior. Sophie would watch and wait.

CHAPTER 12

Joel felt light and hopeful as he left the small hamlet, leaving his daughter safe with Tilly and her mother and traveled east toward where he left Hannah. In one long day, he would get back to the stone hut. It would be three full days and Joel knew how weak she was, so as he traveled closer, he became anxious.

The stone hut was in view looking more desolate than expected nestled in among the tamaracks and oaks. When he approached, he slowed, knowing something felt different. There was no smoke from the chimney. When Joel pushed the door open the stone cabin was cold with the feeling of having been abandoned earlier. The weight of the silence lay heavy. Joel entered and turned, feeling the empty chill of the one-room hut. No sign of Hannah. Or of anyone else who has been there recently. He pushed despair aside. There were things needing to be done before he began his search for Hannah. Joel calmed down after the initial shock of the empty cabin and tried to think. He sat where once Hannah slept. Finally, as night fell, he left the hut to find firewood and fresh water at the small stream.

Joel gathered wood, built a fire in the stone fireplace, made tea and rested. He slept for hours on the pallet where just days ago he held a weak, exhausted Hannah.

Early the following morning Joel arose, searched the area, found nothing new or unexpected, continued to pile wood and keep the shack warm. In the hours that followed, he set snares, caught and roasted a couple of hares. The stream grew wider a distance downstream from the cabin where Joel plunged his hands deep in icy water to capture small fish by noodling them from under rocks. Wet and cold, he took his ketch to the cabin to cook over the spit and to dry himself out.

When Joel was not looking in ever widening circles around the hut for any clue about Hannah, he prepared food for travel. Joel knew Hannah, surely still very weak, would not travel north, plodding up the steeper hill on the wider track, she would not have the strength, so he concentrated his search west toward the creek and south, back the way they first came. To the east, behind the cabin held heavy woods. Joel could not begin to know what the woman might be thinking, if anything rational at all, but doubted she would enter a heavily wooded area.

A week had passed when Joel decided he could do nothing more here. Feeling empty but not knowing what else he could or should do, Joel took one last look then headed for the track that led west. He would go fetch his daughter. Or would he? He felt conflicted, knowing the baby was less than a fortnight old. His daughter was safe with the woman, a wetnurse, a new mother. Joel shook off concern and felt a certain lightness knowing his daughter was being loved and fed, an excitement he did not expect to feel enveloped him. His daughter would surely still need the woman who gave her nourishment, a new life. A life he and Hannah could not give her. Still, she was Hannah's daughter and she had family - a father and grandmother who loved and needed her, wanted her.

Joel pushed his pain aside and felt more hopeful than he had in days. The track did not look familiar in the morning light, it had been very early and cold the morning he carried the baby away from her mother. That was on the third day of her life. She felt so small and still, held close inside his coat. He and the child were near death when he finally saw the candlelight in the window of the distant cottage. That very night he met Tilly and her mother.

Now, on a clear dawn morning, as he followed the same cart trail, he felt sure this lane was the right one because there was no other roadway turning west so near where he left Hannah, so Joel walked on.

As the sun rose Joel felt he must be at least halfway to where he left his daughter. As he rounded a bend, he saw something ahead. Drawing closer, he could see it was an old man, setting at the side of the road with his hand on the handle of a cart full of wood. Joel hastened to see if the man was ill or injured.

The old man seemed startled seeing Joel jog toward him. He shrank back.

"Are you hurt or sick?" Concern on the young man's face could be clearly seen. The old man visibly relaxed. "Well, I'd have to say not hurt, just too old to get any farther just now." Pulling on his beard, he looked down, shook his head, knowing he was admitting defeat. He looked up extended his rough, weathered hand, "Name is Peterson, John Peterson, and you would be?

"Joel," nothing more as the young man decided to set for a moment with the old man and his loaded cart.

Joel felt the need to travel on and get to the village before the day grew dark, still he forced himself to settle and rest. He was sure this was the right path but not sure how much further he would have to walk before reaching the house where he left his child. He hoped the old man lived near where they sat, and that he knew the countryside. Thinking back, Joel remembered he had reached the edge of the village after a long day, and arrived after sunset, but he felt much stronger now and the weather held fair. Maybe he was closer than he thought. He looked at the weathered face of the aging man. His aged hands hung limp, too tired to move just now, Joel knew he could not leave the old man on the side of the road and walk on.

"Do you live near?" Joel turned his head to glance around where they sat and could see no sign of a building.

The old man nodded and looked off to his left, "Just yonder, not far. I just forget I'm not as good at this wood fetching as I used to be."

Joel could not hold back a smile, "I have to go farther before nightfall but let me help you get this home."

As Joel stood, he extended his hand to help the old man to his feet before he pulled the loaded cart in the direction the old man pointed. After just a few minutes, he saw a small cottage nestled in the birch. The two men were approaching a small, covered porch where they were met at the door by an elderly, rather stocky woman in a long apron, "Well, glad to see you home again, Mr. Peterson, and I see you have found a nice helper." Turning towards Joel she said, "Very good of you to bring my man safely home. I have roast and potatoes on the fire, so come and be welcome for our noon meal."

The woman smelled of fresh baked bread. Joel thought of his mother and home and felt the sharp pain of homesickness.

Joel glanced toward the path leading to the road, knowing he must go soon, but Mr. Peterson prevailed on him to stay, enjoy a good filling meal.

"You can be on your way shortly." Joel agreed to sit with the old couple and share their meal, a small delay before he would then go fetch his daughter. Joel felt anxious to be on his way, but the old couple seemed so glad for his company, and the food smelled delicious, so he stayed.

During the meal, Joel asked many questions and John told him about the village just ahead. "I have a good friend there, the blacksmith, Piper Trask. Piper, if you need help, he would be your man."

"I'll remember that." Joel felt sure a blacksmith could not help him on his journey. Still, in leaving, he shook hands with and thanked the old man. "Thank you for everything."

John said, "We will be thanking you, and wishing you safe travels, take care." The old man lowered onto a wicker chair on the stoop and smiled.

Mr. Peterson assured Joel he would reach his destination late in the afternoon. The young man set off taking long strides to collect his child.

Joel reached the outer border of the village late afternoon only to find the cabin where he left the baby with the woman and her daughter, Tilly, empty. Cold and empty. Not yet evening Joel walked to the closest cabin, some distance away. His knock was answered by a woman wiping her hands on a long apron., "What is it you need, Sir?"

Joel wasn't sure where to start. He pulled the cloth hat from his head and asked about the family from yonder stone dwelling.

She smiled, "Oh, those lovely people left. Yes, they left some days ago. Just packed up their cart and their two daughters and went someplace farther west." The woman paused. "The nice neighbor said they were going to be near her man's elderly people, help care for them and all." The woman smoothed the apron and pushed back the bun of graying hair, "I miss that little Tilly, she would run over or wave often. She laughed at everything," pausing she continued, "and she adored her little sister, Lilly."

Joel stood, hat in hand, stunned. Gone! The family left to move further west with his daughter. With his daughter. Lilly! The lady called her Lilly. Joel thought of the crude little talisman stamped with a rough drawing of a lily. Perhaps the woman who took Lilly from Joel and kept the child alive and safe understood the importance of the small rosary with the crude fastener hooked to the little one's blanket.

Joel thanked the woman, turned to leave before turning back to ask, "How long have they been gone?"

Rubbing her chin in a thoughtful way, "Well, they left out early one morning before daylight. It took them a day or maybe two to load the cart. Her man returned home and spoke of going farther west. He always seemed a careful sort and took his time packing the cart." The woman twisted her lips, touched her cheek, thinking, "I guess it was three, maybe four days ago." She looked up at Joel, "Does that help? Were they your kin?"

Joel tipped his cloth hat, "No, just folks I knew." Joel walked away, fighting tears, surprised to feel them damp on his face.

Joel slept out under the shelter of a stand of oaks, waking early the following morning. Disheveled and full of nameless pain, he once again approached the home of the neighbor he spoke to last evening.

"Sorry to bother you again but do you know which direction my friends traveled? Did they say how far they would go?"

The lady looked puzzled for a moment, trying to remember, then pointed to the western end of the village, "I watched them leave out that way, that Tilly bouncing along side of the cart, the little one turned to smile and wave before they passed out of sight." The neighbor looked down before looking off to the west and smiled, "I will miss my friends, especially Tilly."

The woman paused before adding, "The blacksmith, Mr. Trask at the forge was a good friend of theirs. He probably knows where they went." She pointed to the west end of the street.

Joel nodded his thanks and strode west to the blacksmith's lean-to. With one horse and a loaded cart, along with two small children, they would surely travel slowly. His confidence grew as he reached the forge. A big man stepped out to greet Joel, and the young man extended his hand, asking, "Are you Piper Trask".

The big man stood silent until Joel mentioned John Peterson, "He said you were friends and might be able to help me."

"He did, did he. Well what kind of work do you need?"

Joel stuttered, not knowing quite how to start. Then he straightened and just told the truth. He asked about the family with his daughter and where they might be headed.

Mr. Trask stood silent for long minutes, before saying, "The folks you are looking for are my friends. They'll be found west a distance from here across the river." Speaking slowly, looking at the ground from time to time, Mr. Trask spoke, "The spring runoff has the river up some, a bit higher than usual. You mind if we take a couple of horses and I go along with you. Might need to check on my friends, make sure they got to where they were going. They've had it rough this past year. I'd sleep better if I knew things were good with them."

Joel was stunned. The offer of a guide, a companion, along with a horse. He held back tears hoping the blacksmith didn't notice, finally saying, "I cannot pay you."

Mr. Trask turned and was off to get ready, with a chuckle he muttered, "Pay not needed." Before saying over his shoulder, "I can be ready within the hour."

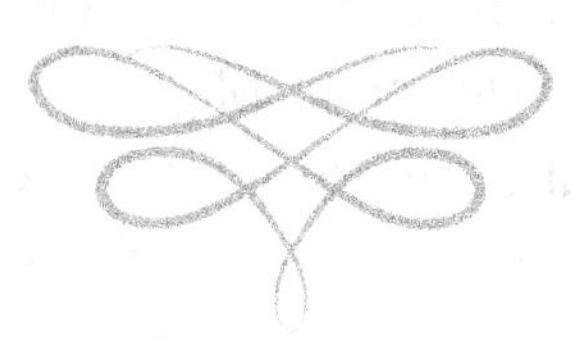

CHAPTER 13

Later that morning rain fell in a heavy downpour as the two men left the small village but Joel, mounted with Mr. Trask at his side, was determined to keep a steady pace no matter what the weather. They noticed on their second day from the village that small waterways were flowing higher than expected.   Both men were soaked through and finally found an overhang large enough for a fire where they hoped to dry out.

So far, this trip felt like a new low even for Joel. He could hardly think or feel, knowing his completely miserable life slowly became even more worthless. If not for John Peterson telling Joel of his friend Piper, the young man was not sure he would have struggled on. Could Piper Trask be another miracle?

As he warmed and his clothes began to put off steam, Joel let his thoughts wander to the beginning. Back to the days full of youth and lust for life with Hannah. Ah, Hannah, beautiful Hannah. His thoughts shifted to the last time he held her, no longer beautiful. Gaunt after the grueling night, and the birth, with little rest, no nourishment.

Hannah, exhausted from giving life to their daughter, had given all that was left to give. No way to bathe or comfort his red headed girl, his love, who gave all she had to him willingly and may have given her life along with all the rest. Joel shook himself, "No, Hannah is not dead I would know, surely somehow, I would feel the loss. And our daughter lives, I know she does!" Joel, now warm and comforted by his thoughts, closed his eyes and slept.

Mr. Piper watched the tormented young man across the small fire, seeing the obvious distress, a dark aura hung over him.

As dawn broke, Joel opened his eyes to the new morning and could see the day held clear. The incessant rain finally decided to cease and show the men a little kindness. Joel walked to the swollen river, filled his waterskin and returned to the small cave to make tea. Roots were available and the hot tea lifted their spirits. Piper smiled, "Today we will figure out how to get across." Joel looked doubtful.

The men followed the rushing river north. As the sun moved past the noon hour, the two men stopped to rest and take notice of the terrain around them. The landscape changed, now there were low hills in all directions. The river continued to rush by, when suddenly Joel looked at debris in the river, "What is held in that yonder pile of debris?" At first glance he thought it nothing more than a beaver dam or just branches in the river. Looking closer he could see a body floating in among the branches. A man. A man's body probably drowned trying to cross the swollen river. Joel pulled the body free and drug him up the bank. Hard to tell how long the man had been dead. It was not the first time Joel encountered a dead person, but this was different, and Joel considered what to do next when Piper came up alongside Joel and gasped.

Joel turned, "What?"

"This is my friend, Tilly's father" Piper slumped to his knees.

Shocked at the situation, all kinds of scenes ran through Joels mind. Where was his daughter? Could the river have claimed her, too? Joel slumped to the ground near Piper, head bowed in sorrow, when he felt Piper getting to his feet, "We've some work to do here," and he lifted the body. Joel looked on. Piper carried the body up the slope and stopped by a tree, "This will have to do, my friend." He spoke as though Joel were not there. Joel gathered himself and went to help Piper bury his friend.

After they finished the work of putting Piper's friend to rest and marking the grave, the man touched Joel on the shoulder, "Time to go see about the others."

Joel knew he was right, this would not be the time to grieve, there would be time for that later but not today. Where were the others? The woman and the two children? Were they drowned too? Joel looked at Piper, thinking, 'he is one of the strongest men I have ever met', and something new shifted in Joel, the young man, no longer a boy, and perhaps not yet the man he hoped to become. But something changed, and for the better. Joel felt the change. He followed Piper along the riverbank, staying alert. Traveling west, then north, Joel noticed the river seemed much smaller, narrower, now than just a league or two back.

Catching up to walk beside Piper, "The river has changed."

Piper nodded.

Piper stopped to point, "back there aways, the river widens when two smaller streams flow together, one from the north and one from the northwest." Piper turned, lowered his head in thought, "This branch is from the northwest. We'll be able to ford it up here, not far now."

Joel watched the river flow out of sight, "Then how far to your friends?"

Piper smiled, "Not far. We should be there by nightfall."

Joel was not sure how he felt. He stooped to grab his knees, felt his body tremble. Was he ready for whatever lay ahead? What would they find once they arrived at the home of Pipers' friends? Was his daughter there, alive? Piper's friends were now his daughter's new family. How would they receive him, the father that seemingly abandoned the infant? Joel shook himself, forcing the dark terror to leave, at least for now. He felt an unfamiliar emptiness as he remounted.

The village came into view in the late afternoon and Piper pointed, "There. They live just there, in the larger house".

The two men saw candlelight in the windows as they approached. Once on the porch, Piper knocked, and the door opened almost instantly. An elderly woman said, "Oh, I thought you were the doctor," Then she stopped, looked at Piper, "Oh my soul, Piper, so glad you have come." She turned to enter the house before saying, "How did you know to come?"

Piper turned to introduce Joel, "My friend is on a journey, and I decided to come this far with him."

The woman looked puzzled before she shrugged as she looked Joel up and down before speaking, "Oh dear, where are my manners." She then led the men into the room where an old man sat, obviously blind.

"Charles, Piper is here. He just came with a friend."

The old man extended his hand, "How did you know to come? Well, no matter you are here now.

The girls are here. They thought Ty might have been lost at the river, but we've had no word." He stopped to lean back and let his head slump forward as he took a large kerchief and dabbed at his eyes.

Joel heard and looked for any sign of children. He listened, thinking, 'the hour grows late for the young ones so if they are here, they are probably in bed for the night.'

Piper needed to share grim news, "We found Ty's body on the riverbank and buried him there."

Piper and Joel heard the gasps before the old man spoke, "A man from our village found our daughter-in-law and her babies and brought them here."

The woman sat bent, weeping, as the old man continued, "It has been a sorry thing. The healer may come again today to check on Tilly, but Ty's wife, and the baby have been taken where they will get the care they need. The son's wife is not well."

Joel held his breath, so they were here and now gone but his baby is or was, still alive, at least until recently. He waited, wanting to ask where the woman and child were taken but held his silence. Piper asked, "Where is Tilly?" The old woman said, "Come quietly. She is sleeping now and we are so grateful. The fever seems to be leaving and she can finally take broth." The men stood at the door of the small room and watched as the little girl slept peacefully.

Returning to the larger room they sat at the table while the old woman ladled stew into bowls for the men. As they ate, taking turns talking, the old couple shared their story. "The neighbor brought Ty's wife and two children here one afternoon, late it was, a couple days ago. A sad lot, they were." The old man added, "No word of our son, Ty."

The old lady looked at Piper, adding, "Ty's wife grew worse with a fever, something the healer was not familiar with, so he decided we needed to make arrangements and send her off to the castle a distance to the north".

The conversation stalled as the men ate. The men pushed back from the table when the old woman finally added, "It took some doing but we had a cart and a driver soon enough and we bundled them up the best we could." Looking at Piper, she added, "We don't expect to hear anything for some time."

It slipped out before Joel thought, "When did they leave?" Before adding "Where is this castle they were taken to?"

The old woman looked again at Joel, the same sharp eyes taking in the young man for the second time. "Would you be knowing our folks?"

The blind old man, now back in his comfortable chair offered, "They were taken by neighbor Brown to the castle just north of here." Pausing, rubbing his chin, "They would be there by now. A few hours up the track to the north."

CHAPTER 14

Ty's mother held quiet before saying, "The castle is a-ways up through those hills to the north, and we hated to send them, but we knew we did all we could do. We knew the daughter-in-law needed more help than we could give. The healer came often but didn't seem to help. The castle folks come this way from time to time and told us to come see them if we ever had need."

She paused, "So we decided to do just that. We sure hope they get there in time. The babe seemed well but Ty's woman was weaker by the hour, and the babe still nursing so we sent them both." Tears flowing, "I hope the babe is not with fever, too."

As the conversation continued, Joel could hardly contain his need to start north. Piper watched Joel, seeing the young man's internal struggle, his need to be moving, to be on his way. Piper understood.

"Maybe you could ride on ahead, find the castle. I will come and meet you there in the morning." Joel nodded, gave Piper a grateful look and excused himself. Through the night he rode north hoping to find a castle and his daughter.

CHAPTER 15

The days were warm, and the flower gardens were beginning to bloom. Those close to Max knew he was in love with the redheaded woman, Hannah. "The man whistles all day long and never stops smiling when he is with her." They knew Max and knew his smiles were different, this time more personal.

Some said they would marry soon; they were sure of it. When asked, Mary Elizabeth said nothing. Only she and Abba understood Hannah's true pain.

No, Hannah would not marry, at least not yet, not until she was sure all that she loved was truly lost. Mary Elizabeth felt concern for Hannah, but she could not forget her friend Max. She loved him, as many others at the castle did, were drawn to the quirky man with the quick wink and smile. But there seemed no way to avoid the hurt that could come without warning.

Hannah felt stronger each day and recovered her health during the lengthening spring days. She laughed and talked with Max often when she was not immersed in a book or enjoying the presence of women friends. But the shroud of sadness never completely left her. Perhaps Max found the allusive sadness part of the fascination surrounding Hannah, a cloak of mystery. Mary could not say, but she wanted the best for both of her friends.

Hannah continued to come when called to help with any task, especially when Mary asked for or needed help. Hannah talked with Abba and tried, truly tried to find peace and be happy.

One evening while resting on a bench in the garden she was startled by the appearance of Max. He sat beside her for a moment before slipping to his knees, "Hannah, you must know how I feel." Max smiled, revealing his dimples, the sparkle in his eyes. "Will you marry me?"

Hannah seemed startled, confused, "Oh. Max, you don't really want to marry me. In truth, you do not know me."

Max stopped and slowly moved again to the bench, "I have never been surer of anything in my life." Smiling, revealing his dimples, eyes shining, "I'm serious! Marry me."

Hannah was thoughtful, silent, knowing she loved another. Tears slid down her cheeks. Now Max seemed confused, "What is wrong? Hannah, please talk to me. Maybe I can help."

Hannah touched Max's hand, "You have been and are my friend." She stopped looking down before she raised her eyes. Meeting his gaze, Hannah told Max her story, all of it, and why she could not, would not marry. She could not forget her first love, Joel. And the thought of her lost child was a pain most difficult to carry. Max heard it all, first he felt shocked, then confused, before the reality of Hannah's world, the reason her sadness remained, never really leaving, and the reason she wept so easily became apparent to Max. Max let Abba's love change his heart. He did not, could not, fully understand, but he knew his feelings for Hannah were strong, just different. Max began to understand.

Hannah still mourned the loss of Joel and her baby. She hoped Max could understand. Somehow,

Hannah felt responsible, she should have been stronger, made Joel stay with her and somehow kept their baby close. The memories would never set her free to have a new different life. Hannah felt tears fall, her bodice became damp as she tried to explain all of it to Max. Holding her face in her hands, she knew she did not want or need a new different life. Max leaned in and brushed a strand of hair from her face. His face softened, a mixture of compassion and love and sorrow filled him.

Hannah lifted her face to look at Max and knew he understood. She never meant to hurt her friend. And he was a true friend. The perfect person for Max would come in time. It just could not be her.

Later that day Hannah sought out Mary Elizabeth who suggested they speak to Abba. "He will guide you, perhaps show you the best way to move forward. If your man and child are indeed lost to you forever, then the castle will keep you safe and, over time, bring healing." Mary stopped, thoughtful, remembering something Abba shared earlier. "The beginning sometimes brings surprising endings." Hannah understood that Mary saw and heard things others could not fathom. Much like Abba.

Not understanding how, or why, Hannah was comforted by Mary's words.

As she and Mary Elizabeth approached Abba in one of the side gardens, color in so many hues from pastels to deep reds and purples filled their senses. Hannah's heart lifted and she knew in her heart that if there was an answer, Abba would have it and would guide her.

Abba seemed to be waiting for the two women when they found him resting in a quiet place in a small side garden. As they talked and Hannah shared her story with these people, most of it already known, Abba listened before he shared his feelings. He advised Hannah to breathe and do nothing at all. Looking deep into Hannah's eyes before taking her hand, he said, "All will come right, I am sure of it. Time itself has a way of making a crooked way straight. Just breath, trust, and live a good life one day at a time,"

Mary Elizabeth stood, said 'good-bye' and Hannah followed, not sure what just happened, but Hannah knew she felt more positive than just minutes before.

On their way to the lanai for tea, they were interrupted, someone coming quickly down the passageway, and when near they called for Mary Elizabeth, "Could you come." The caller spoke softly but clearly.

Mary asked Hannah to go on alone and wait for her. She would join her for tea as soon as she could, hoping whatever this emergency would not take long. Hannah needed time alone since her meeting with Max and then her talk with Abba, so she agreed to wait for Mary, take time to sort out her private thoughts. Much of her heartache seemed to have lifted. Though nothing in her world really changed that hour, Hannah felt a new serene hope.

CHAPTER 16

Joel topped a ridge and looked across the long low valley, seeing the huge castle with walls and gardens as far as the eye could see. The front portico could be clearly seen. He stopped, held his horse in check, afraid to stay in place, but felt too unsure, possibly afraid, to approach the massive structure. His ride through the night left the young man exhausted, perhaps to be expected since the journey to find his daughter filled the past few days with a since of loss, sorrow to this point. Hoping to hang on and stay atop the horse for another mile, he nudged his mount forward, riding through the trees to the front steps of the castle.

Joel sat still for long moments, mounted and unsure. A man wearing livery apparel with a companion stepped out of the side entrance to inquire if the rider wished to come in. Joel said he was there searching for his infant daughter. "I think she arrived a few hours ago in a cart with an ill woman." Both men shook their heads, having seen nothing.

The men helped Joel dismount and welcomed him into the castle.

Once inside, and weary, Joel looked down at his worn and soiled clothing and felt uncomfortable. One of the men who brought Joel in left saying, "I will return shortly with someone who can help find your daughter, if indeed she is here."

In a few minutes, a tall, lovely woman approached.

Mary Elizabeth came quickly when called and sent for Henri, not sure what the trouble was. When they reached the front of the castle, they encountered a young man, slumped against a corridor wall, holding his face with his hands. Two men stood near and lifted their hands to signal Mary when they noticed her coming down the corridor.

Mary spoke softly, "Take him to one of the resting chambers, I will be there shortly." When Henri arrived, Mary shared what little she knew about the man just brought into the castle and they followed the two helpers to a quiet room. Mary looked around, making sure everything was as it should be, "Henri, the room is warm enough. But perhaps someone should bring in more wood for the fire."

Hearing this exchange, Joel startled those gathered near when he said, "No, no need. I cannot stay, I will rest later. I will rest once I have found my daughter."

Straightening, the young man repeated, "I have come to fetch my infant daughter. She arrived with a sick woman a few hours ago in a cart and I believe she is here."

The tattered young man, stood, head tipped as tears etched down his face. Mary watched, feeling the man's pain as though it were in some way attached to her.

"Come, I promise we will find your daughter if she is here." Just then Bridget came, whispered something in Mary's ear.

Mary's countenance did not change as she turned to look at Henri, hoping he understood, then to the weary young man, "Please rest while we get to the bottom of this for you." She turned again to Henri, "Take good care of our new visitor. I will return shortly."

The exhausted man was wrapped with warm blankets and leaned back to rest in the care of Henri and two friends, Bridget and Darla, while Mary quietly left the room.

Bridget smiled at her friend, Henri, "Really no need for you to stay, we will stay here." Henri agreed, thanked the thoughtful women and left saying he would stop in later. He touched the young man on the shoulder, "Rest for now while we get the answers you seek."

When the weary young man tried to rise, Bridget touched him gently on the shoulder, saying, "You are safe here and we will help you find what you are looking for, but you must rest. Just until Mary returns, please." Joel knew the little woman was right. He lay back and closed his eyes.

Under her gaze, Joel closed his eyes and relaxed under the warm blanket. He would trust the little woman, Bridget, and her companion, Monika, and the one called Mary Elizabeth, and enlist their help as soon as he felt stronger. He would rest, but not long, until he knew all there was to know concerning his daughter.

Darla smiled, whispered, "I will get another blanket and more candles." And slipped quietly out of the room.

The man appeared to be sleeping. Thinking she could, Bridget decided it might be a long evening, so she decided to move quietly into the hall and go fetch a pot of hot tea, leaving the young man asleep, warm and safe.

But as soon as Bridget left and was out of sight down the hall, Joel heard the soft rustle of her garments, and realizing he was alone, he stood and stepped quietly from the room into the hallway. The young man felt sure Mary and Henri disappeared down the hallway in one direction, so Joel slipped out of his room and followed.

Mary always went quickly when summoned. She seemed to glide, never appearing to rush even when rushing seemed required. And she complied as quickly as she could. Leaving one task for another.

Just after leaving the room of the father looking for his daughter, this new emergency seemed to have occurred, she was needed suddenly in another part of the castle. Mary remained calm.

She appeared to exude some kind of special joy in being needed and seemed always to have the sought for answer.

A friend met Mary Elizabeth in the passageway, "Come. There is a need, I will tell Abba that I found you and sent you to the quiet room where the small ones are cared for." When Mary entered the quiet room, she seemed pleased to see Hannah leaning over a crib, laying a sleeping infant down, before the young woman turned to ty her bodice, and seeing Mary, the young woman smiled, a peaceful, contented special kind of smile.

Mary watched as Hannah let her hand fall to touch the babe in the basket, looking first at the little one then up at Mary Elizabeth with a look that could only be called completely serene.

"The babe, three weeks old, perhaps a month, suckled vigorously until satisfied, with tiny fists up against my breast to help guide. It's a girl." Hannah, barely above a whisper, seemed mesmerized. "And my breast still held milk, more than enough to satisfy."

Mary smiled, her eyes warm as her gaze rested on Hannah and the sleeping child.

"Who called you, Hannah?" Sophie having just come into the room, looked around Mary to ask Hannah, as both women continued to watch their young friend.

Hannah, still smiling the soft smile, "Abba sent someone for me, said I was needed here."

When Mary Elizabeth, with Sophie following, reached the infants' room, both tried to understand why they were needed. Hannah seemed to have everything under control with the new infant. Who needed who? Just then someone came in to tell Mary she was needed in another part of the castle where the sick was cared for.

A woman was dying. Sophie said, I'll go", but Mary, feeling things others could not, extended her arm to stop Sophie's leaving, before lifting her hand, and spoke softly, "We will all go." Hannah hesitated but Mary assured her that a friend would be in the room to watch over the infant while they were taking care of the sick woman. Knowing Hannah hesitated to leave, Mary turned to look with kindness at the young woman, "Hannah, I need you to come with me." Now Sophie seemed confused. Mary rarely could be heard speaking so directly.

Sophie looked at Mary and saw the odd aura that covered her dear friend at times and knew to step back when she heard Mary speak. The three women left together and moved quickly to follow the one who came to get them.

The three women entered the sickroom where just a few hours ago a very sick woman was brought into the castle in a cart.

Monika stood wringing her hands, "So thankful you could come. We heard the woman who came in earlier was dying. No one seems to have known her, but she uttered something with her last breath and held this in her clutched hand." With that, Monika opened her hand to reveal a small string of beads held with a crude brass clasp. The outline of a lily imprinted on the metal clasp.

Hannah's startled cry could be heard by those present. She crumpled in a faint to the floor.

Sophie and Monika lifted the girl and carried her to a small adjoining room. "I will stay with her, Sophie. Help Mary." Monika covered Hannah with a warm quilt, hoping to comfort her.

When Sophie returned to Mary, she asked, "Who left the woman here? Was she alone?" No one knew the answers to Mary's questions.

"Please find me the person who brought her in." Monika rushed out and soon returned with one of the groundkeepers who shared with them that he indeed was the one who brought her and the infant in. The infant?

The man continued, "The older man driving the cart said he must return to help others and left as soon as he knew the mother and child were safe in the castle." The man paused, "How is the mother and the wee one?"

Mary shook her head sadly and asked the man to wait down the hall, she would speak to him soon, "Thank you for helping."

Hannah slowly sat up and held the cup to her lips as her mind cleared before letting another breath escape; she understood where the baby she just finished feeding came from. The mother died, leaving the motherless child. All Hannah wanted now was to get back to the little one, to hold her, to be sure she was safe. Still, how did the woman come to be holding Hanna's own baby's string of stones in her dying hand? Hanna could not reason out an answer.

When Hannah recovered and entered the dead woman's room Mary turned to Hannah, "please return to the quiet room, to the infant, while we finish here." Relieved at being dismissed, Hannah turned and left quickly.

The myriad of questions swirled through Hannah's head, as she all but ran down the passageway toward the room where she left the baby in the care of others.

Mary and Sophie called for others who would prepare the woman's body for burial. Now finished, Mary was entering the hallway, when she turned to see a stricken Hannah come toward her.

"The babe is gone!"

Mary Elizabeth spoke, "Impossible! Someone was there with the child."

"I tell you the basket is empty, no one seemed to….." her voice trailed off as she chocked and tears threatened.

Sophie came up beside Mary and Mary and Sophie both seemed stunned by the news. "Who would take a baby? Where was the one in charge when the babe disappeared?"

Then Mary remembered. The broken young man recently brought in and settled on a cot to rest in one of the quiet rooms. She remembered he said he was searching for his infant child.

Hannah wept, shaking her head. Monika and Darla stayed with Hannah while the others hurried to the room where they left the exhausted man.

The tattered man who had been resting in the quiet room just a short time ago was gone.

The room stood empty.

The women stood together, puzzled, unsure what direction to take next.

Mary first to speak, said, "I will go and speak with Abba."

Searching for Abba, Mary ran into Max in the hall. Though startled, Mary thought to ask Max if he had recently seen a tattered man leaving the castle with a babe in his arms.

Max smiled and said, "I did. How did you know? He was in a hurry to leave so I showed him the shortest way to the front of the castle and offered to help him find transportation for himself and his child."

Mary listened, tried to put the pieces together, the dying woman, the tattered young man, a nameless infant. She felt her heart lurch, remembering Abba's words. "Do not be concerned, all will come right soon."

Hannah and Darla and the others in the hall heard a commotion. A noise came from down a side hall before Hannah and the others came into view. Max seemed startled to see Hannah with tears streaming down her face too distraught to stop. Mary held her arm out to stop Max from moving and pointed Hannah to the front door. Hannah understood Mary's gesture and ran onto the wide veranda.

Seeing the tattered man down the wide steps, standing in the driveway holding the babe, Hannah yelled. "Stop."

As the young man turned, holding the wrapped infant close, he looked up and stood in disbelief, "Hannah?"

Hannah stopped on the veranda steps, then slowly descended the steps and approached the man holding the child, recognizing first Joel and then seeing the child in his arms.

"You came for her, for us."

Max watched from the castle doors as Joel and Hannah clung to each other and reunited around their child. Mary stepped close to Max, placing her arm around him,

Max looked at Mary, "Ah, you knew, didn't you?"

Mary nodded, "Are you going to be alright?"

Max smiled, letting deep dimples show as his head of curls fell in all directions. "Just another day in castle life, some you win, some you lose, but mostly, you learn and grow." He sardonically laughed, "Abba told me I will have my heart full and running over when things are right."

The two friends turned to reenter their lives in the castle, lives of helping others come in out of the dark into the light, into the warm welcoming castle.

THE END

Epilogue. Joel and Hannah grew from children into parents with not one but two daughters to raise. They were quietly married by Abba in the castle. Later, Hannah and Joel returned to Tilly's grandparents' farm to gather Tilly and her possessions before finding a small cottage near the castle to call home. They promised to visit the old ones often.

Friends from the castle were frequent visitors to Joel and Hannah's home, (including Max), and of course the young family visited the castle often, gleaning wisdom from Abba, and seeing their friends. When Lilly turned five, the small family returned to Joel and Hannah's home in the south to visit parents' and to invite them north to visit. The small village brimmed with joy at their return.

Joel often marveled at how truly incredible their lives were — from young irresponsible love to devastation out in the cold, dark world, to in the end, living near the castle, holding more than enough of all that they could ever want or need.

The End